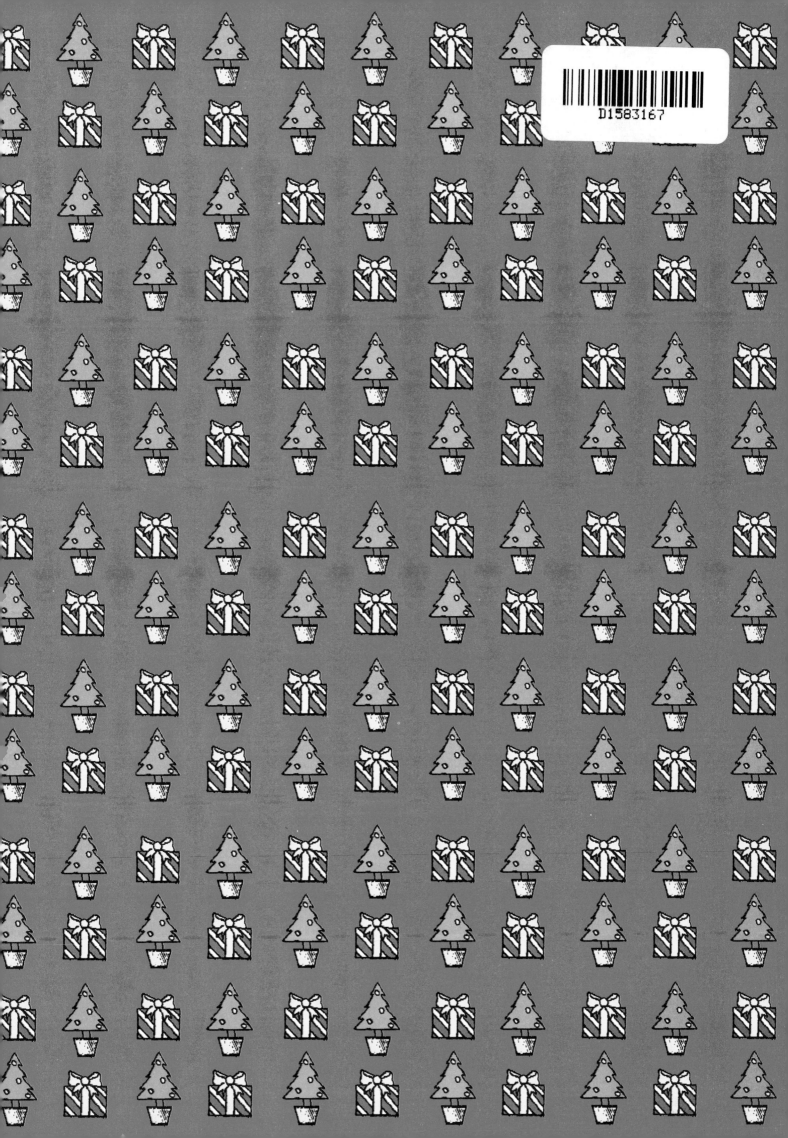

Contents

First Published 2000 by Brown Watson
The Old Mill, 76 Fleckney Road,
Kibworth Beauchamp, Leicester LE8 OHG
ISBN : 0-7097-1341-X
© 2000 Brown Watson, England
Reprinted 2001, 2003
Printed in the E.C.

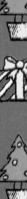

EASY to READ
Christmas Stories

Illustrations by Stephen Holmes
Stories by Maureen Spurgeon

Brown Watson
ENGLAND

Christmas on the Farm

It was a very cold, wintry afternoon at Happydale Farm.

"Soon be Christmas!" said Farmer Merry. "Time to put a Christmas tree in the hall!"

"Soon be Christmas!" said his wife. "Time to cut the holly and mistletoe. I want some big bunches for the dining room."

"Soon be Christmas!" cried Jenny. "Time to make cotton wool snowballs to stick on the windows."
"And make lots of paper snow-flakes!" added Peter.

"Moo! Moo! Moo!" went Buttercup the cow. "Who wants cotton wool snow and paper snowflakes? You get real snow outside, where we are, not inside, in a house!"

"But there are lots of things inside!" said Lenny and Lucky, the two lambs. "Just see!"

"Maybe that's because most of Christmas happens indoors," said Denny the Donkey.

The animals talked about it for a long time. How they wished they could go indoors, just for once!

"People talk about stars at Christmas," said Denny. "They're up in the sky! Look!"

As well as the stars, they saw something else in the sky.
"It's like the sledge that Jenny and Peter play with in the snow," said Denny.
"A sleigh," said Hector the Horse.

"And those are reindeer!" added Denny. "It-it's Father Christmas, the man who brings presents on Christmas Eve!"
"Couldn't we ask him to bring us something?" cried Lucky.

"We don't want presents," said Hector.
"We only want to go indoors to see what
Christmas is like."
"Then that's what we'll wish for!" said
Denny.
"What a good idea!" said the others.

But all that happened next morning was that Mrs. Merry put a sack of straw into her car.

"Come along, Jenny and Peter!" she called. "Time for school!" It seemed very odd to the animals!

The straw was for the Nativity Play which told the story of the first Christmas, when Baby Jesus was born in a stable. Jenny was going to be Mary, the mother of Jesus.

Peter and his friends, Billy and Mark, were going to be the shepherds.
"Baby Jesus needs a manger to lie in," said Miss Lane, their teacher. "What could we use for that?"

"We've got a real manger at our farm!"
Peter said proudly.
"Dad would lend it to us, wouldn't he,
Mum?"
"We could bring Lenny and Lucky to
school, as well," said Jenny.

But the animals were disappointed when they heard the news.
"We all wanted to see Christmas indoors!" said Lucky. "It's not fair, just me and Lenny getting our wish."

"Tell us all about it when you get back!" said Hector.

"Don't forget!" squawked Hetty the Hen.

"I can look indoors," said Denny, "and see for myself!"

Denny could see that Lucky and Lenny did not like being indoors. The children were kind and the play was lovely, but they felt hot and uncomfortable, and they missed their friends.

But Miss Lane was very pleased.
"You have all worked hard!" she told the
children as they got ready to go home.
"Look, it's beginning to snow! Just in time
for Christmas, too!"

It snowed all through the night. By next morning, the snow had stopped, but it was still very, very cold. All the pipes at school had frozen. Miss West said every-one had to go home.

"No Nativity Play today!" she said. "I am sorry, children."

"Oh, dear!" said Farmer Merry. "We've brought the manger and the lambs, too."

But Denny the Donkey had an idea!

He ran down the road, braying loudly. "He wants us to go back to Happydale Farm to do the Nativity Play!" said Farmer Merry. "Everyone in the school mini-bus, Miss Lane!"

Buttercup the Cow, Hector the Horse and Hetty the Hen were surprised to see Denny leading the mini-bus towards the big barn at Happydale Farm. Everyone looked so excited!

"The perfect place for our Nativity Play!" cried Miss Lane. "Change into your costumes, children!" Soon, lots of people were crowding into the barn, waiting for the play to begin.

So, as well as both the lambs, Lenny and Lucky, Denny the Donkey, Buttercup the Cow, Hetty the Hen and Hector the Horse all appeared together in the Nativity Play.

"So this is what Christmas is really about!" said Denny. "I'm glad we could share in it all."

"Well," said Hector the Horse, "that is what we wished for. Don't you remember?"

Not long afterwards, it was Christmas Eve. As the reindeer pulled his magic sleigh across the sky, Father Christmas smiled down at all the animals on Happydale Farm.

He had brought bells for Lucky, Lenny and Buttercup, a basket of straw for Hetty, apples for Denny and a blanket for Hector. How surprised they would be on Christmas morning!

The Little Christmas Tree

Once, on a hill above a town, there was a little Christmas tree.

So many big trees grew all around, there was no room for the little tree to spread its roots, so it hardly grew at all. Nobody even knew that the tiny little Christmas tree was there.

As Christmas time drew near, the little tree always felt so unhappy. He could see people looking at all the other trees and hear the children laughing and talking to each other.

"Ooh, look at that lovely big Christmas
tree. Isn't it great!"
"We can hang lots of presents on those
strong branches!"
"This Christmas tree is so nice and tall!"

"Choose me!" thought the little Christmas tree. "Please choose me!" But nobody did. Then, one cold winter's night, something happened. Quite suddenly, a strong wind began to blow.

The wind howled down all the chimneys, blew under all the doors and rattled all the windows. And it whistled through the branches of all the trees, tugging hard at the roots.

The little Christmas tree held on for as long as he could. But then a sudden gust of wind blew hard against the bottom branches and he felt himself being lifted high into the air!

"Whoo-Whoo!" whistled the strong wind, blowing harder than ever. Only one person saw the little Christmas tree whirling and twirling about on that cold, snowy night.

Gradually, the wind died down, as more big, white snowflakes fell from the sky. The little Christmas tree felt himself falling, falling, until he came to rest on a bed of snow.

"About time, too!" came a voice, and a figure in a red cloak and big boots picked up the little Christmas tree. "You always wanted to be a proper Christmas tree, didn't you?"

Little by little, the sky became lighter and a pale sun shone down. "Hey, here's the Christmas tree we wanted!" someone shouted. "Mum said Santa would bring it, Jason!"

"Let's take it indoors," came a boy's voice, "then we'll find a big flower pot or something and fill it with earth. We'll soon have this looking like a real Christmas tree!"

"I'm glad it's a little Christmas tree!" said Anna. "Big Christmas trees need lots of decorations!"
"And it's tall enough for me to reach the top branch!" laughed Jason. "I like it!"

They worked very hard all morning, cutting out paper stars, making balls of silver foil and hanging things on all the branches. The little Christmas tree loved every minute!

There were lots of games and parties and fun around the little Christmas tree! Someone caught their sleeve on a branch and a piece broke off, but the little Christmas tree tried not to mind.

"Our poor tree!" said Anna.
"All its little green needles are beginning to fall off."
"That always happens," said someone else. "Christmas trees don't last long indoors!"

By the time Christmas was over, the little Christmas tree was very worried.
"We'll put all the decorations in the cupboard ready for next year!" said Mum.
"Any rubbish for the dustmen?"

"What about the Christmas tree?" asked Jason. "We can't put that in the cupboard."

"No," said Mum, lifting the Christmas tree out of its flower pot. "It will have to go outside."

The poor little Christmas tree trembled so much that a whole shower of green needles fell to the ground. He was taken outside and set down by a cold wall, waiting for the dustmen.

After a while, the little tree was lifted up
again – but he hardly cared. All he had
ever wanted was to be a real Christmas
tree. He had never been so unhappy.

He began to dream that he could hear birds singing, just as they did when he had been with the other trees on the hillside. He thought he heard a voice, sounding just like Jason.

"Look at the birds! They're eating all the food we've put round our tree!" The little Christmas tree looked down at his new, green branches, with the birds darting in and out.

"That little tree has certainly brightened up our back yard!" said Mum.

"You always said nothing would grow, because we don't get much sunshine!" said Jason.

"But we really don't want our Christmas tree to grow!" said Anna. And all through the months that followed, the birds would come and perch on the tree, chirping and singing.

As the days grew shorter, the time came for the birds to fly away to warmer lands. But the little Christmas tree did not mind. Soon, he knew, winter would come once again.

Then he would be a real little Christmas tree again, with stars and silver balls. Anna and Jason loved him. "Because," said Jason, "we can have a little bit of Christmas all year round!"

The Magic Reindeer

Ronnie the reindeer was always in trouble! "Oh, Ronnie!" cried Mother Deer. "How did you get your antlers tangled up in this holly bush?"

"Ronnie!" roared Stag. "Why must you charge through the stream and splash water about? Look, I'm dripping wet!"

But as soon as Ronnie saw a bird in the sky or leaves rustling on a bush, off he'd dash. Then it would be, "Ronnie! Don't tread in our water!" or "Ronnie! You've splashed us with mud!"

All this made Ronnie feel very sad. If only he could do something really special, he thought, something to make all the other reindeer really proud of him...

Ronnie tried hard to think what he could do. But long after the other reindeer were asleep and night had fallen, he still hadn't thought of anything. He gave a big sigh, looking up at the sky.

Father Christmas was out on a practice sleigh-ride, ready for Christmas Eve. But Ronnie didn't know that. He was watching the reindeer flying! If they could fly, he told himself, he could, too!

Ronnie began practising the very next day. Off he went to the top of a hill. He took a deep breath, ran as fast as he could, then jumped, flapping his hooves about and hoping he would fly!

But flying wasn't nearly so easy as it looked! Ronnie just fell to the ground, squashing a clump of lovely, fresh grass! "Ronnie!" roared Stag. "You're getting into trouble again!"

Ronnie tried all sorts of things — hopping about on each hoof, jumping up and down... being so busy and moving about so much, he hardly noticed the snow which had begun to fall.

And this time, before Ronnie could make a jump, his back hooves slid on the icy ground. Up he went into the air, his legs moving all at once. Ronnie could hardly believe it!

When Ronnie landed in the soft snow, he could see that he was quite a long way from where he had jumped – and that could only mean one thing! "I can fly!" he cried. "I can fly!"

It was so exciting, Ronnie didn't want to stop! Again and again, he tried sliding on the snow, then lifting up his hooves and sailing through the air! "Look at me!" he cried. "I'm flying!"

Some of the other reindeer had already
seen him! Off they went to tell Stag and
Mother Deer about Ronnie learning to fly!
But someone else had seen Ronnie, too...

"Oh, no!" groaned Father Christmas. "That little reindeer down there is trying to fly! And I thought everyone knew that only my reindeer can fly across the sky!"

Just then, Ronnie took another jump, flapped his legs and his hooves about, and fell down – thump!
Poor Ronnie! He could not help grinding his teeth in pain!

"I must do something about this, "Father Christmas decided. "Steady, my reindeer. Let me get a sprinkle of stardust!" Soon, he knew, Ronnie would try to fly yet again.

Sure enough, the little reindeer ran over the snow. Then he lifted his legs, tucked in his hooves, and... Whoosh! Up he flew into the sky in a shower of magic stardust!

With stars twinkling and the moon
shining, Ronnie could see all the trees
and bushes, now far, far below. A cool
wind blew on his hooves and his legs,
until they didn't hurt at all.

"Oh," said Ronnie, "now I know how it really feels to fly!"
"You had worked hard, trying to learn," said Father Christmas. "You deserved to have your Christmas wish come true."

By now, the other reindeer had called Stag and Mother Deer.
"Ronnie? Flying?" roared Stag. "Rubbish!"
"If he's got into trouble," said Mother Deer, "I'll ..."

But none of them ever knew what she would do. Because, at that very moment, the moon came out from behind a cloud, making all the deer look up into the starry night sky.

"It's Father Christmas!" said the reindeer.
"And his reindeer sleigh..." added Stag,
almost in a whisper.
"And Ronnie!" cried Mother Deer. "He
really can fly!"

Father Christmas guided his sleigh behind a mass of white, snowy cloud. "Time for you to go, Ronnie!" he smiled. "This moonbeam will take you safely home."

Sliding down a moonbeam was as much fun as flying. "Oh, thank you, Father Christmas!" cried Ronnie. "I hope I see you again!" "You will, Ronnie!" laughed Father Christmas. "You will!"

Ronnie landed safely on all four hooves. Now Stag, Mother Deer and all the reindeer wanted to hear about how he had flown with Father Christmas across the starry skies!

And if he slid on the snow, or fell in the mud or trod in the water, nobody minded too much. They were all so proud to know such a clever, wonderful, splendid reindeer like Ronnie!

Santa's Busy Day

Santa had been busy all morning, getting ready for Christmas Eve!

"Have a rest, Santa!" cried an elf. "You're always so busy!"

"But I like being busy!" said Santa. "And do you know the job I like best of all?"

"Riding the sleigh!" said the elf. "Putting all the toys in the sacks!" cried the little Christmas Fairy.

"Wrong!" laughed Santa. "What I like best is reading all my letters."

"Your letters!" cried the little Christmas elf. "That reminds me! Has anyone written asking for a little wooden engine, Santa? This one gets left behind every Christmas Eve."

"I don't think so..." said Santa. "Can you put it in my sack? I really must read these letters. They're from children in the town I'm visiting tomorrow!"
Suddenly, he stopped.

Dec 20

"Listen to this!" he said.
"Dear Santa, will you please bring an extra nice present as a Christmas surprise for our daddy. Thank you. Lots of love from Tina and Tom!"

"If only Tina and Tom had said what they wanted for their daddy!" groaned Santa. "How do I know what he would like?" "What about some hankies?" said the Christmas Fairy.

"That doesn't sound much of a surprise!" said Santa. Then Penny Pixie, who helped to look after the reindeer, had an idea. "What about one of your Christmas beakers?" she said.

Santa Claus gave a big smile. "Now that's a real Christmas surprise!" he said. "I can't wait to see Tina and Tom's faces when I meet their daddy tomorrow!"

Very early the next morning, Santa got ready to begin his long journey. "Wrap up warmly!" said Penny, tucking a scarf inside his cloak. "You're sure to have a very busy day!"

It was still dark when the town where Tina and Tom lived came in sight. "Put me down beside that big Christmas tree," Santa told the reindeer, "and then you can take the sleigh back home!"

Soon, Santa knew, he would be busy meeting people and hearing what everyone wanted for Christmas! He was looking forward to seeing Tom and Tina with their daddy.

He didn't have long to wait. "Look, Daddy!" someone cried, and a girl and a boy came hurrying up. "Tina and Tom!" smiled Santa. "Here's that Christmas surprise for Daddy!"

"We're Mike and Mandy, not Tina and Tom!" said the boy. "And I'm Paddy, their big brother!" said the man. "But thanks for the surprise, Santa! It's just what I've always wanted!"

"Oh, no!" thought poor Santa. "What can I give Tina and Tom's daddy, now?" Just then, up came another boy and girl, with someone wearing a crash helmet and motorbike leggings.

"Come on Tom!" cried the girl.
"Tom!" thought Santa. "Tom and Tina
with their daddy!" Without thinking, he
unwound the scarf from inside his cloak
and handed it across.

"Here's a Christmas surprise for you, sir!"
he cried. "A very merry Christmas!"
Tom gave a cheer. "Just what Sam
wanted!" he cried. "She looks after us."
"Sam?" echoed Santa Claus.

The person took off the crash helmet with a shake of her long, fair hair. "A scarf!" she cried. "Just the thing when I'm riding my motorbike, eh, kids?" And Sam gave Santa a big kiss!

So many people wanted to see Santa Claus on that busy day! Everyone looked so pleased and so happy, he could not help smiling. But at the same time, he was also very worried.

Santa had been so busy, giving out lots of lovely things from his sack, that soon there would be nothing left at all!
"Oh dear!" thought poor Santa Claus. "Whatever shall I do?"

"Hello, Santa!" someone said, and Santa Claus turned to see a girl in a bobble hat. "I'm Tina and this is my brother, Tom! Did you get our letter about a surprise for our daddy?"

"Er, well..." Santa stopped, and without thinking, he put his hand deep into his sack, feeling around at the very bottom. There was something small and hard, tucked away in one corner.

It was the little wooden engine! Tom and
Tina's daddy gave a big smile, reaching
out to touch it.

"A model engine!" he cried. "I've always
wanted one! Thank you, Santa!"

"You are clever, Santa!" said Tina. "Tom said you'd know what Daddy wanted!" Tom looked very proud. And their daddy? He just kept looking at the little wooden engine!

Santa was chuckling all the way home! "Why did I worry about that Christmas surprise?" he kept saying. "I only had to remember that grown-ups never quite stop being children!"

It was soon dark. Snow began falling and
Santa was glad to see the lights from his
workshop.

"I'll be glad to have a rest!" he told his
reindeer. "I've had such a busy day!"

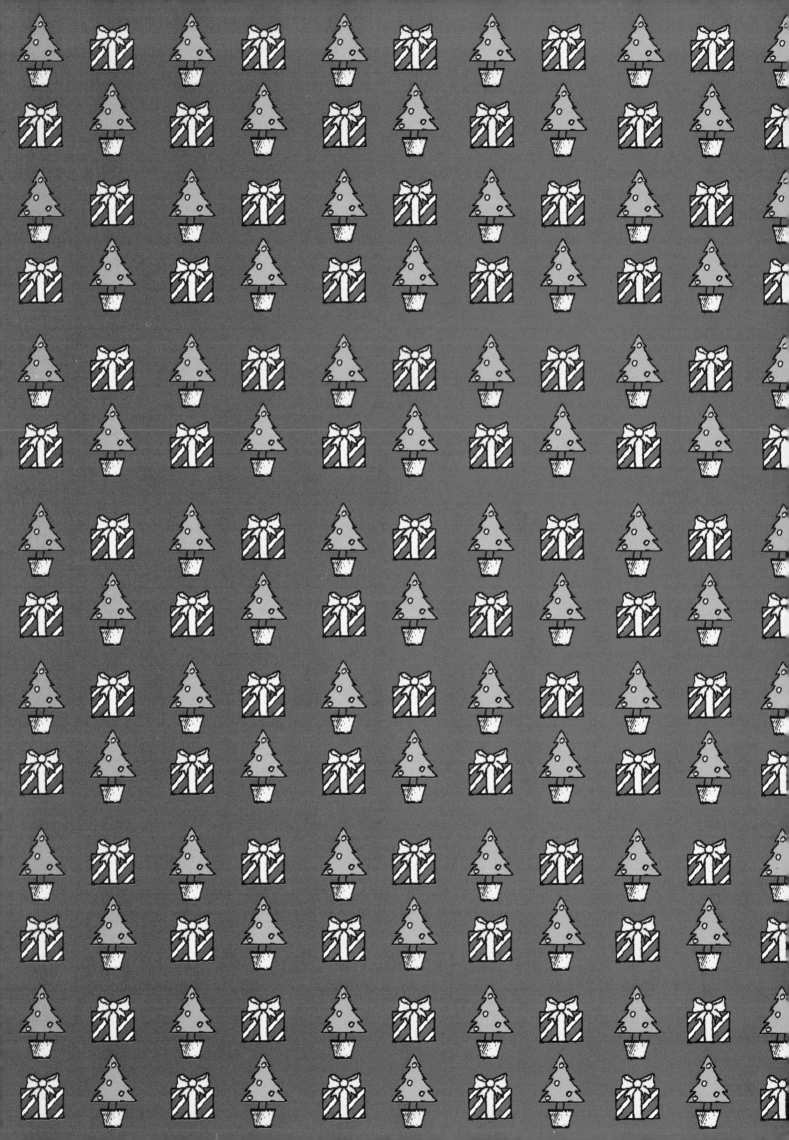